Black Shadow

by Jay Eisenhofer and Mark Eisenhofer

Illustrations by Christina Cartwright

ISBN: 978-0-359-94446-0

The best characters are a little bit
good and a little bit bad.

Mark Eisenhofer, age 7, 2017

Chapter 1

You know me as Black Shadow. It's not my real name of course but that is how I am known across 115 galaxies. Anyway, most of what they say about me is not true. I wish I could say it's just the bad parts that are false but a lot (most?) of the good parts are not true either. My real name is Terrence Moor-Yamalon. Everyone calls me Terry. This is my story. All of it is true. So when you hear the story told by someone who heard it from someone else who heard - well, you get the idea - you will know the truth.

So, Black Shadow. It's funny how I got that name. After all, I'm technically still a kid. I say technically because the Intergalactic age for adulthood is 18 and I'm only 17. But I have been on my own since

I was 14 and took off from the Home for Unwanted and Unruly Brats (not the real name of course) on the planet Xaralien. But that is another story for another time. And one thing I have a lot of right now is time. I am sitting on my cot in a 4 by 8 cell with a tiny window the size of the postage stamps from the 20th century they keep in the History of 2 Earth Museum at the Zoran 25 Spaceport.

I know I should blame Lata that I'm in here but I'm

blaming Dr. Z. Even though he doesn't know I'm here (and would really like to know). You know his famous line? "I gave up Science for Crime." If he had stuck to science, I would not be here. Of course, if Lata hadn't been so cute, I definitely wouldn't be here.There are two guards outside my cell that look like giant Rhinoceroses except they are standing on two feet, not four. And they are carrying electric blaster guns. They keep snorting at each other so maybe they are part Rhino. And they mumble in some dialect I have never heard before. When they grunt directions, spit flies out of their mouths. I just hope none of it gets in the food they serve although food might be a nice term for the gruel they give us here.

Anyway, I was telling you about how I came to be known across 115 galaxies (I know, I know, that's the entire known and charted Universe - I was paying attention in geography class - but 115 galaxies sounds better) as a master criminal and all around bad guy. And did I mention that there is a price on my head (I know, a reward for my capture - I wasn't paying attention in Grammar class - boy was that boring and there was a very cute girl - Cathy something - sitting just at the right angle across from me so I could stare at her all through class and there was no dress code and - well, you get the idea).

As for that creep who ran the place - Mr. Alberto- if you are reading this - know that I am coming for you - eventually. Right now, you are number 5 on my list, but number 1 in the Quadrillion Sector so when I am in the neighborhood - you will be seeing me. I know you are supposed to let bygones be bygones but a grown man in charge of children shouldn't be slapping them around and picking on them. The last time he went to hit my friend Runt I grabbed his wrist. He actually looked happy I was doing that like he had been waiting for his chance.

He said something like, "Now you're going to get it." That's the last thing I remember before I took my pen and jammed it in his ear as hard as I could.

I heard him screaming as I went out the window. That's the last time I saw that place. I hope Runt is ok. Maybe I should move old Alberto up the list - maybe number 3 - and make a special trip to the Quadrillion Sector. I have to get out of here first, of course.

"Hey," I shouted to the Rhino guards, "When do I get my call? I know my rights as a citizen of the United Union of Galaxies. Even here on Prestis 3, you have to follow the rules of the Union." What a joke, me talking about the rules of the Union. But hey, whatever works. The Rhinos just grunted at each other, not even looking at me. They probably know I don't have anyone to actually call.

But back to the price on my head - 20,000 Gold Debits! Now, that may not be a lot compared to Dr. Z or Blizzard - I think they get 200,000 - each. But not bad for a 17 year old kid who until two months ago was using a stolen license to fly in and out of space ports. How did I get my own space cruiser? Another story for another time. Or maybe just later in this story.

And as for Dr. Z and Blizzard - I am not one to name drop but I do know them. Well, not, know them, know them, as in we never hung out together. And they wouldn't recognize me or even know my name. I do have something they want although what it is, I have no clue because it makes no sense to me. It's a computer disk with a lot of numbers and letters on it that make no sense, which right now is sitting in a locker at the Space Train here on Prestis 3. If I get shipped to a prison planet, I can kiss that disk goodbye. Of course, I'll have bigger problems if I end up on a prison planet. Like being surrounded by slobbering Rhino-people grunting at me for twenty years while I slave away in a prison mine. But let's look on the bright side. Is there a bright side?

Okay, enough of that. How I came to be known as Black Shadow with a price on my head. And by the way I've been told it's a very handsome head although one problem with being 17 and on the run across 115 galaxies (I'm not going to say Known Universe - that sounds like a travel show) is that it's not easy to meet girls. Most 17 year old girls don't want to introduce their boyfriends to their parents by telling them that he is a smuggler and bandit - even if he is a very good one. Like, this is my boyfriend - Black Shadow - you can call him Black for short? Uh - huh - not happening. Now, I have met a few older girls (I know if they're older, they want to be called women, not girls). That worked out nicely a couple of times except for Lata, of course. I will never trust another redhead. Or anyone named Lata. What was it Jack Lightsky used to say? Oh yeah, "guys do stupid things for pretty girls." I should have listened. Again (I know you're getting tired of hearing it) a story for another time.

Just then, the Rhinos opened my cell door. I thought it was so I could make my call and I was trying to come up with someone - anyone - in the Known Universe - to call. I started to say, "It's about time" when a human (except for his nose which looked like it belonged on a Rhino - do they cross breed here?) in a white lab coat entered my cell. "Routine intake procedure" he mumbled as he took out a gauze swab, one needle, and a vial. "Please give me your arm" he said, swabbing a spot and then jabbing my vein with the needle, filling the vial with blood.

"What is this about? When do I see someone? It's really a mistake that I'm here."

He didn't even look at me. I wanted to grab his arm but I saw the Rhinos watching me. Their skins looked like it would take a double phaser laser gun to even prick the surface, so making a fuss was probably not a good idea. The Rhino nose human left and they closed the cell door. I could swear the nose and Rhinos grunted and talked to each other. Does nose talk Rhino?

How did I get myself stuck here? Well that's really the same story as how I came to be known as Black Shadow. Let me start at the beginning. It's actually because I am smart - or supposed to be - or was when I was five years old. Let me explain.

Chapter 2

I am an Intellicon. If you don't know what that is, you are lucky. When I was a little 5 year old, living on the planet Crystal - Z with my parents and going to kindergarten, one day a year was reserved for testing. A kindly looking woman with grey hair came into the classroom and smiled and handed out test booklets. Don't worry children, she said, just relax and do your best. It isn't important how you do. We just want to see how much you have learned this year.

Now when I imagine that scene, I see the words coming from her mouth in flames. And snakes coming out of the test booklet.

You see, 120 years ago, the leader of the Union,

Zoran I (we are now on Zoran IV), realized the most

precious commodity in the Universe was now

intelligence. So, he decided to locate and find and

train all the smartest children in the Union. Then

they would marry each other and produce more

smart kids. All of whom would be trained to run the Union and be loyal to Zoran. At first, they sent kids with high scores on their tests to special schools. But since they were still living with their parents and hanging around with non- Intells, they weren't getting with Zoran's program fast enough. So, Zoran decided to take kids from their parents right after they test them at 5 years old if they score high enough. That's right - just get them out of their houses and ship them across the galaxy to special colonies where they would live with each other and their instructors. And never see or hear from their families again. Of course, I now know that isn't even the worst part. But let's save that for later. I know - how can that not be the worst part? Believe me, you'll see how.

You might think Zoran would be an unpopular guy for doing something like taking kids from their parents. Well, he isn't. He has kept the peace - the Union hasn't had a war with the Space Barbarians for a hundred years and there is hardly ever even an attack on a Union planet that isn't one of the outer territories. And people keep getting richer. Life is always getting better. I think that's Zoran's motto or theme song or something like that. Anyway, that is definitely a story for later.

Now my parents were pretty ordinary. But they were special to me. And I didn't appreciate being hauled off to some special school on the planet Beltran that felt like a prison camp just because I was smart. I say it felt like a prison camp but it was supposed to feel like summer camp.

Our camp was called Liberty Shades and it was a pretty place. Miles of rolling, green hills with paths for biking and hiking. Lakes for swimming (and heated pools). Basketball and tennis courts.

Airball fields. Even a golf course. The dorms were nice also. Children ages 6 - 10 lived in 3 bedroom apartments with an adult proctor. From 10 - 16

you shared a 2 bedroom with another Intell. After 16, you could get your own place or have to share. It depended on how you did. We called the kids with their own places "the toadies". All the apartments were nice - not luxury like in the magazines- but nice furniture, advanced electronics and a game room filled with age-appropriate games. The school had the best teachers and they and the proctors were all very nice to the kids. So, once you got over missing your family and friends, it was supposed to be nice - like I said, like a fancy summer camp. With people telling us all the time how important we were to the future of the Union. How special. What great things we would do and what great lives Zoran would make sure we would have. How lucky we were to have been designated Intells.

But you say, I said I was an Intellicon. And yes, that is different from an Intell. You see, most Intells get with the program - Zoran's program - either right away or eventually. They have a whole routine to get them over being separated from their families. At first, they don't even tell you that's what's happening. They just make it like you are going on a special vacation for very special kids. By the time you get the idea you aren't supposed to care because you are living in paradise and being trained to save the Universe. Zoran rules the Union and everyone knows the entire Universe would be a peaceful place if only the Union could be extended to rule the rest of the Universe. Especially the Mineral Belt - but more on that later. Well, I tried to get with the program. I wanted to be a good little Intellibot (as I came to call them) and grow up to be a good toadie. But something held me back and kept getting in the way. I just

never felt quite right there. The nicer they were to

me, the nastier I got. I had temper tantrums when

I was seven. When I was eight, I got in fights with

other kids. When I was nine, I got in big trouble for

throwing rocks at a party of toadies. Hey, why did

they have a party in a field surrounded by trees that made it easy for me to hide? Of course, I thought I was hiding, but that was when I found out that we were under almost constant video surveillance with hidden cameras all over the place. Ten and eleven were a lot like eight and nine. Fights, getting in trouble, the start of not listening in school. A lot of sessions with kindly counselors who tried to figure out what was bothering me. Actually, I was having a great time. The counselors got more and more serious over time. And sterner. And started to warn me about how I didn't want to fail. I had been given this great life - the Keys to the Kingdom - I shouldn't squander it with stupid misbehavior. I agreed. I really did. But I was kind of having too much fun breaking the rules and seeing how much I could get away with. And so when I turned 12, I came

up with a plan for some real fun.

Once I figured out about the cameras everywhere,

I knew I was going to have to do something about

it. It kind of gave me the creeps, knowing they

were watching our every move. I used to talk

about it to see if it upset anyone else but no one

really seemed to care. Or at least they acted like

they didn't. They would just shrug or say

something like "Isn't that so they can keep us

safe?" Or, "It's for our own good?" Or, "What are

you trying to hide?" I didn't understand why I was

the only one it bothered but it just bothered me

more and more that no one else cared.

So, whenever I got the chance - for a couple of

years - I learned about the video system. How

could I do it? Well, not everyone at La La Camp

(my nickname not theirs) was an Intell or a teacher

or administrator. You would have better luck

getting blood from a stone - as they say- than info

out of one of the teachers or admins. I truly think

that they were afraid that Zoran would hurl a

lightning bolt at them or some such thing if they so

much as raised their voices to question anything.

But what they forgot was that there were a lot of

other nameless, faceless workers at the Camp.

The kitchen staff, the cleaning ladies, the

maintenance men, the landscaping crews. Most

of the students didn't even notice they were there -

it was if they didn't exist. Others were polite and

even friendly. Some knew some of their names.

Some even knew all of their names. But very few

of us - maybe no one - actually talked to these

people. Even the campers who knew the names only used them politely - as in Thank you John. Excuse me, Mary. May I have another piece of cake, Linda. Can you get me a new whatchamacallit for my room, Harry. No one knew anything about John, Mary, Linda or Harry or the dozens of others who lived outside and worked at the Camp.

So, you didn't have to be a genius to figure out that they might respond if someone took an interest. And that's what I did. I talked to them - not about what they were serving for lunch or how tasty the cake was - but about them. Where they lived - their families - their kids - especially their kids - and where they were from. By the way, no one was actually from Beltran. We had all been brought there - kids - teachers - workers. And so,

I became the little darling of the staff. Not everyone. Some were suspicious. Some wanted nothing to do with any of us, having decided we were all brats, no matter if we were nice or rude. Others were just too terrified - they had nightmares of being punished by Zoran with a sentence of space exile where you roam the galaxy in a space pod all alone for years under the control of a computer that issues you just enough daily food to keep you alive forever. They say that Zoran II got sick and his wife, Harakline, came up with that one while he was ill. I was never sure if people thought that Zoran was a good guy and anything bad was someone else's fault. Or if they just cut him some slack because a guy can't run half the Universe and know about everything that's going on, can he? Or did they figure it was someone else's problem and you have to be tough to keep the peace and keep the money flowing.

But back to my plan. I had made friends with a lot - not all- of the camp workers. I hung around with them. I helped them. I talked to them and listened to what they had to say. And I occasionally made off-hand comments about the video system. And little by little, I found out things. I found out that the video system controls were housed in a room separate from the main building. I could watch it with night goggle binoculars. No, I do not own a pair. Yes, I lifted them from the science lab when our goofy science teacher was answering questions after class. So, maybe I do now own them, after all.

One thing Liberty Shades definitely taught me is that ownership is really another word for possession. If you don't own anything then maybe you own everything. Or vice-versa. Jack Lightsky would have laughed at that one. His take on it was simple - take what you want before you get taken.

Anyway, I watched the video headquarters with my night goggles a lot. I wasn't sure what I was watching for or even what I could do if I ever got inside. And then it came to me. Using my night goggles, I had learned the security code to get inside. But it did me no good because there were always two people inside. One guard and one operator. Most nights that was Harry and Mac. The one thing I knew they had in common was that they lived near each other in Sector 6, a workers' residence area. And you may say it was a cruel thing to do and hey, I'm not proud of it , either. But it worked.

I lifted one of the teachers - yes, the spacey science teacher who was always distracted by the attention he got from students crowding around after class - all because they were either brown nosing him or didn't understand a word he had said - so, I lifted his phone from his desk after class. And that night after dark, I sent a message from his phone to the Camp emergency hotline that there was an electrical fire in Sector Six and people were trapped. Then I forwarded the message to the video headquarters. Alarms sounded immediately. It sounded kind of like you imagined it would if the planet was under attack. Loud ear splitting sirens, everyone running about, most of them only half-dressed. Everyone trying to remember what they were supposed to do but no one knowing what was actually going on. Except Harry and Mac. Thanks to me, they knew.

And they knew their families were in danger. So they locked up the video room and got into their vehicle and hurried to Sector Six to try and protect their families.

I calmly entered the video room after they left. From there it was easy. The system was not set up to be secure because after all, what did they have to worry about from a bunch of kids who all want to become good little toadies? So, it was a snap for me to find the feed for the daily morning message from our esteemed Camp leader - Dr. Prexydile - or Pretzel as I called him - and replace his boring good morning, dare to be great with 100 Pretzel sucks, repeated over and over. Then I left, leaving no trace I had ever been there. And of course, I wore gloves - I know about fingerprints.

So, the next morning, Pretzel started off his

message to all the happy campers by informing us that last night's sirens and emergency had been a mistake and they were looking into it and would know the cause very soon. Then came the pre-recorded message of the day complete with the usual video of Zoran, Union headquarters, the Camp, our smiling toadie wannabe faces and even some juicy scenes of life in Capital City where every guy is married to a model and every girl looks like a model. But today, the video had a banner across it that said Pretzel sucks and just to make sure no one missed the point, the audio repeated that message over and over. I had left the uplifting music in the background. I kind of liked the effect of that coordination.

Well, it only took about thirty seconds before they took it down but it sure did cause a commotion.

Campers - teachers - toadies - all were buzzing. All were horrified - shocked - some were visibly shaken that their little world had been disturbed. As if the Union itself had been invaded by the Space Barbarians.

Me, I felt pretty good. Like I had pulled a private joke on the entire Universe. Unfortunately, my private joke only stayed private for about thirty minutes. There I was in my History of Mars class silently smiling about my own brilliance when two guards opened the door, whispered to the teacher and escorted me out of class. Thirty minutes! Some master criminal.

The next thing I know I'm facing Dr. Pretzel, across his desk in a huge office filled with pictures of Pretzel and a bunch of different political figures. I think there was even one with Zoran though that one was a group of six guys, not just Pretzel, with the great one. All of them with their faces so red and shiny like they were next to the Lavalline System Triple Sun itself.

Pretzel didn't waste any time. "Are you familiar with DNA," he asked me. I was a little bit although clearly not enough. But I could see right away where this was heading. And it wasn't good for me. Pretzel explained that Camp LaLa had a DNA registry of every camper and that mine was found all over the video control center. He then recreated my entire crime for me - from lifting the Science Dork's phone to the false report to the video tampering. He even seemed a little impressed that a 14 year old could have pulled off the whole scheme. I didn't think there was anything to be impressed about - I had gotten caught, hadn't I? And fast too. If it was so impressive I wouldn't have been sitting there staring across the desk at Pretzel, wondering how many days of detention I was going to get. I figured for this, it would be a lot - a month, maybe even two. But when I heard the actual words: Xaralien… Attitude Adjustment Program… a Year… Reevaluate… Hope you can return… I wasn't feeling so brave any more. I had heard about Xaralien - where they sent Intells who were socially maladjusted. I always thought it was a myth - make believe - like the bogeyman or the devil or the six headed snake monster from Venus III (which by the way, is no myth but more on that later).

So, I packed up my things - Barely enough for a

suitcase. And off I went. Xaralien. Home for

wayward Intells. The ones who didn't appreciate

how lucky they were that Zoran had given them

the chance to help him save the Union.

Ungrateful, selfish, maybe just no good. Or, as I

called us: Intellicons.

Chapter 3

So that's how I got there. Now for how I got out of there. But first, a little - a very little, about Wayward Brat School.

It didn't take me long to see that the real purpose of the place was to make everyone so miserable, they would beg to go back to Liberty Shades. Also, a lot of the kids weren't really bad kids, they just hadn't been able to cut it at Camp Intell. Like Runt - he wanted to be a good, little Intell but he had trouble keeping up. So Alberto picked on him and picked on him some more. Is there a reason people in charge like being mean so often? Were they mean before they got put in charge?

The other thing I saw as soon as I arrived was that

no one really went back to Liberty Shades. That was a story they told us to make us feel better.

No, Xaralien Brat Camp had another purpose. I didn't know what it was but I decided not to hang around long enough to find out. I started planning my way out right away.

Then Alberto picked on Runt one time too many and next thing you know, I was making a very unplanned getaway. When I was walking - OK,

running - across the field on Xaralien,, there were two things going through my mind. One, was get out of there as fast as possible before the planetary police - and worse the Volchinks - arrived to arrest me. Have I mentioned the Volchinks? Zoran's elite force. A combination police, army and spy force. They patrol the cosmos and operate on every known planet.

But back to running. And two, how was I going to get home to Crystal Z and my family. I knew I needed to get to the city as fast as possible. Once I was there, I could try and hide out among the crowds. And I could try and figure out a way to get a lift out of the Spaceport. The sick feeling in my stomach told me I didn't really believe either one was possible. Not with the Volchinks searching for me. I thought for a second that just

maybe they would let me go and not bother

looking but I knew that was a pipe dream. I didn't

just run away. I stabbed a teacher with a scissors.

Of course, the creep deserved it but they wouldn't

see it that way - no sense of humor, those people.

Then I considered returning to the school and

throwing myself on their mercy and begging for

forgiveness. But I knew that wasn't happening

either. I was never going back there.

The school was surrounded by woods, farmland and a semi-deserted highway. Not the best landscape for making an escape. Only the woods provided any cover. And, about those woods. They were a dark mass of gnarled and twisted trees and thick bushes. There were no paths. You would have to fight your way through and around the trees and poisonous plants spread throughout.

And then the animals. Everyone knew the ground was covered with venomous snakes and vicious biting creatures called Rapdors were there as well. As if that wasn't bad enough, there were swamps filled with quicksand but covered with leaves so you could step on a pile of leaves and find yourself drowning in quicksand. The word at Intellicon High was that over the years there had been six different escape attempts through these woods. Six times someone had entered the woods. And not once had one of the six made it out.

So, I was not eager to be number seven. I did not want to go into those woods. But I knew it was my only chance. I turned around to look at the Camp. It seemed quiet and all looked normal from the outside but I imagined the inside was very different. In my mind, I saw inside those halls and saw people running about, sirens going off, security pulling their weapons together and calling for their vehicles. People were hysterical, upset and furious with me. Soon the sky would be filled with sky-cabs looking for me. I saw it all as clear as if I could see right through the walls of the school. And I knew it was only a matter of time before the Volchinks showed up. When I turned back around, I knew I had no choice but to go on in. To the woods.

So in I went. Taking small careful steps. Looking all around. Tapping the ground for quicksand swamps before taking a full step in any direction. Looking nervously for any sign or sound of a Rapdor. And that's when I heard the first sirens. Not imaginary ones - real, blaring sirens. I knew what they meant - there was a full-scale search party of Volchinks setting off to find me. Rapdors, snakes and quicksand aside, I had to get moving. So, I started running. I had no idea if I was even running in the right direction. It was so dark I couldn't be sure I was even heading in the right direction. For all I knew, I was running back towards camp.

Well to make a very long story short, or at least shorter, I made it through the woods. No Rapdors, no snakes, poisonous plants or quicksand.

Whether those other six had really survived, I can't say but I have a strong suspicion. From there I made my way into the City by waiting for night and following the canal. Sky-cabs buzzed overhead constantly, shining their spotlights, but the bank of the canal was hidden from view. I guess they thought no one would walk through the murky, smelly, knee-high water. But I did and I exited the canal into the City before dawn. I smelled like someone had dumped a toilet on my head but at least I was in the City. Lots of people, lots of buildings, lots of places to hide. I had one plan – okay, you couldn't really call it a plan – get to the Spaceport and get off Xarlian.

As you can see by now, I'm no philosopher. I do know it pays to be lucky and oh boy did I get lucky hanging around that Spaceport. Because that was where I spotted Jack Lightsky. Of course he was easy to spot. The Spaceport was filled with buttoned up types and soldiers and workers moving cargo. One look at Jack Lightsky was all it took to know he was none of those things. His hair was pulled into a ponytail, and he had a

mechanical right arm. He wore only black with a
purple scarf around his neck. Most striking of all,
he had a large gap in his teeth where he had lost a
tooth and not replaced it that looked like a cave
when he opened his mouth. Oh, did I mention

how loud his voice was? It carried across a room
voice was? It carried across a room or field. From
the first time I saw him, I knew he was my ticket
out.

Chapter 4

But before I go further with how I got off of Xaralien, I think it's time I filled you in a little about Dr. Z. I would say he's the villain of the story but bad as he might be, I'm not sure he's the worst of them. I mean, we're talking Crusher, Kittes, Vankenson, Blizzard, Crystal and of course Lata herself. Eenie, meanie, mineie, moe, who's the worst of all?

So, like I said before, Dr. Z's most famous line is, "I gave up science for crime." Before he became Dr. Z he was Dr. Assenius Zenothopis from the planet Red Earth 14. As you probably remember it was only thirty years ago that the only way ships could get around the Universe was by finding a Dark Seam and transporting through the seam from one end to the other. Now these seams are everywhere - well, not everywhere - but every

planet seems to have at least a couple. And for

years, everyone thought this was the fastest way

to get around. Enter the seam and exit at the

other end somewhere on the far end of the

Universe. It wasn't very efficient because then you

had to travel to wherever you wanted to end up.

And you could only do that at light speed, just like

in the old days. Well, Dr. Zenothopis, as he was

then known had a better idea. He figured what if

you can exit a Dark Seam without going to the

end? And figure it out, he did. With his invention,

ships could all of a sudden transport to anywhere

along a seam. It revolutionized air transport. He

won all kinds of awards and made lots of money.

But it wasn't enough. Just when he was at his

most famous - people were already calling him Dr.

Z but back then people smiled when they heard

that - he dropped out of sight.

The rumor was he was working on teletransport without Dark Seams. But everyone knows that was impossible. Right? No one had ever come close to getting that right. And believe me, they've tried.

Scientists, businessmen, governments. They all wanted to do it. And now that Dr. Z has gone rogue, they need to figure it out. The first time anyone had any idea Dr. Z had invented this device and had become a bad guy was in a casino on the planet Vegastopia 23. He and Vankenson and Blizzard and Crystal walked in and pulled out their double phaser laser guns. Did I mention that Dr. Z's other speciality was weapons? As you know, laser guns are illegal everywhere in the Known Universe since the time of Zoran I. Only Volchinks have them and only a few Volchinks have double

phaser lasers. One of the casino guards tried to

use his electric zapper to stop the robbery but

Vankenson aimed his laser gun and fired and that

guard now has a mechanical hand.

How do I know this? Because it was all on the

casino security system and anybody with a video

connect (in other words everybody) could watch it later. They didn't even use masks.

Some of the workers hit the hidden security buttons that alert the Volchinks. And they do have laser guns. And there are a lot of them. They got there fast. Even before Dr. Z and his helpers had finished stuffing their suitcases with cash. They surrounded the casino with rings of troops. They all had weapons. Then they announced that Dr. Z and his three helpers should give themselves up so they wouldn't get hurt. Dr. Z just waved to the cameras. The Volchink leader said he was giving them 5 minutes. Dr. Z said thank you and the four of them grabbed their bags of money and jumped in their ship in the middle of the casino floor. They closed the ship doors and as the Volchinks came running into the casino, the ship disappeared. No one could find a trace of them. One second they were there and then they weren't. Scientists said it was impossible that they were still alive. Couldn't be done. A week later we found out they were alive. They did the same thing to a Government repository on the other side of the Universe. Then a series of banks, hotels, more casinos. All over the Universe. They were hauling off millions every other day. It went on like this for months. No one knew where they'd turn up or when. They jumped all around the Universe, from solar system to solar system. They clearly weren't traveling by Dark Seam. It was now very apparent that Dr. Z had done the impossible. He had created a way to teleport ships, pinpointing spots in the Universe. No one could catch him because no one else knew how to do it.

Imagine Zoran's reaction to this. Here he is the most powerful dude in the whole Universe - not to mention the richest. He has tens of thousands of scientists working for him. The smartest people on every planet. Money is no object.   And some measly scientist working on his own had solved the most difficult scientific problem in history.

I've heard that Zoran has quite a temper and this got to him big-time. He blew up at his science advisors and fired most of them. He blew up at his chief spies for not being able to find Dr. Z and fired most of them. He created a huge project to discover the secrets of teletransportation with all the so-called best scientists in the Union. In fact, I think that Zoran brought in almost every Humanoid scientist from the Union Galaxies. For those of you who have been asleep for the last four hundred years, Humanoids are basically human robots. They have chips surgically implanted in their brains. That is a surgery that became popular in the 21st century on Earth. After a few hundred years, it was hard to tell the humans from the robots. The first Zoran was the first to use them as soldiers. In the outer Galaxy wars, he defeated the Barbarians using Humanoid troops. But when he became President, he banned the Humanoid operation and wiped out all but a handful of them even though they had been responsible for him coming to power. It was said he had technology which allowed him to monitor and control all remaining Humanoids in the Union. And except for a few who were rumored to have escaped to the Outlands Galaxies, those were the only known Humanoids.

But, bottom line, they were all geniuses since they were basically part machine. Creepy, I know. And if they were all so smart, how come Dr. Z who doesn't have a chip in his brain, was the one who kept inventing all this stuff?

Meanwhile Zoran knew he had a problem that was a lot bigger than Dr. Z just making off with millions any time he felt like it. People all across the Universe - in particular, the rich ones who had a lot to lose, were questioning whether Zoran could keep their money safe. Not just the business owners who had been robbed but everyone felt nervous that any time he felt like it, Dr. Z could appear from nowhere and walk away with as much of their money as he wanted. And these were Zoran's people - the ones he had always kept fat and happy. Now they were terrified. Zoran pushed his scientists to work harder and faster. A few of them cracked from the strain. Another thing that is important to our story. And again not yet, not yet. He pushed his spies to find where Dr. Z was hiding but that is like looking for a speck of dust floating through space.

And then it stopped. No one knew why. No one had come close to catching them. No one had any idea how to catch them. And then there they were back where they had started. On Vegastopia

23. But then all the Volchinks left the planet. They were replaced by men working for Crusher, one of the most notorious criminals in the galaxy. You can figure out how he got his nickname.

Now, just about the only time anyone sees Dr. Z is in his glass box at the Cyborg airball games.

There's still a reward on his head but if Zoran wants to catch him, why did he pull the Volchinks from Vegastopia 23? Did they make some kind of deal? Everyone knows that Dr. Z has used his device to take over and make himself boss of the two or three hundred crime syndicates in the Union and even the civilized part of the Outlands. Vankenson, Kittes, Blizzard and Crystal are his lieutenants. Crusher handles security. They are called Dark Justice. Zoran seems to leave them alone and they seem to leave him alone. In fact,

there is even a security force field around

Vegastopia 23. That could only come from Zoran

since the only other place in the Universe with a

full planetary force field is Zoran's home planet,

Capitol City. The rumor is that Zoran arranged a

meeting with Dr. Z on some Nether planet in the

middle of nowhere and they made a deal. Dr. Z

could be the crime lord of the Universe and be left

alone and safe on Vegastopia 23. In return, Dr. Z

wouldn't use his teletransport to commit crimes.

Of course, now that he is the most powerful criminal in the Universe, he doesn't need to. Zoran promised to make sure all the crime bosses - who are scattered all across the Universe, each with a few dozen planets under their control - would respect the deal.

One thing Zoran didn't promise was that he would stop working on a teletransport device. In fact, the rumors out of Hobotian, where his scientists are working, are that they may be close to improving on Dr. Z's invention. The rumor is that they may be able to create a device that enables people to transport themselves without a ship! If Zoran had that and Dr. Z doesn't (and Zoran won't be giving it to him, you can be sure of that), Zoran would have a leg up on Dr. Z big time. Well, Dr. Z heard these rumors and what he did about it has a lot to do with our story. Just not yet. I know - you are

getting tired of hearing that In the meantime,

though, Dr. Z and Zoran seem to have worked

things out. Even though neither of them has

admitted it.

The whole thing seems awfully smelly to me. Kind

of like the breath from a Rhino prison guard on

Prestis 3.

Chapter 5

Speaking of smelly Rhino prison guards, before I continue with my story, maybe I should bring you back with me to Prestis 3. Back to my dark, tiny, smelly cell. Or maybe to the line of prisoners shuffling to the Yard for a few brief moments of sunshine.

If you stepped just slightly out of line, you got a Rhino grunt and a jab from the blunt end of their electric zapper. At least they didn't just zap you. That was reserved as a threat if you got really out of line.

I watched them zap somebody in the Yard one day. They told us to get moving back to the cells and this one guy – we called him Tiny because he was – guess what – giant sized – he didn't move fast enough. So they grunted for him to move faster and he told them to bug off in so many words. Two of them went at him from different sides and they each zapped him. He looked like cheese melting the way he turned and twisted and collapsed. That wasn't good enough for them though. They kept going even while he was lying on the ground. Then they just grunted and left him there in the Yard like a puddle of flesh.

I didn't like the guy. I didn't even know the guy. I'm sure Tiny was a giant creep. But the whole thing made my blood boil. I wanted so much to

turn those zappers right back on the Rhinos and watch them beg and whine. Well, I can dream, right?

What I did do was go back and help Tiny up. And help him to his cell. It was like dragging a mountain. I had a sore shoulder for a week. I was the only one who helped him though. He might still be laying there if I hadn't.

The guards gave me dirty looks but the other prisoners looked away like nothing had happened. I'm sorry I couldn't just leave the guy there. Not that I cared what happened to him. As I said, I didn't even know him. And as Jack Lightsky always said, "Rule no. 1 is look out for no. 1." That's a good rule but there's something about people (are the Rhinos people?) pushing people around who are defenseless that gets my blood going.

Just like Mr. Alberto who I have not forgotten and will deal with as soon as I get out of here, get to the locker, get my ship and so on. Does that mean I have a different rule no. 1 than Jack? I have to think about that one.

It did make me realize that I was probably pretty lucky the day before. I was standing in the food line looking at the disgusting slop they call food. It was brown and liquidy and looked like it should have a colony of bugs living inside it. There looked to be two alternatives: brown slop or white (actually grey) slop.

So, of course when they grunted at me which did I

want, I had to answer - "I'll take the steak, medium rare." The Rhino never looked at me and grunted like I was speaking some strange language he had never heard before. I said, "No steak today? I'll take the roast beef. Or maybe a nice piece of fish, grilled with some butter sauce. Sweet potatoes on the side? Grilled asparagus?"

His next grunt sounded more like a snarl. "Okay, I'll take the brown slop. Looks a little better today than the grey slop."

Rhino server slopped a heap of stinking brown gloop on my plate and with a nod of his head and a grunt indicated I should get a move on as I had wasted enough of his precious time. I saw him look over at one of the Rhino guards by the wall for just a brief second. He didn't grunt and his eyes barely flickered before he was back to waiting on the next fortunate customer.

I was a little surprised that as I exited the line the Rhino guard against the wall walked by me. He didn't seem to even notice me as his eyes were looking off in a different direction. But as I crossed in front of him, his elbow swung into my tray, knocking my food to the ground. My brown slop was now on the floor - where it probably belonged all along.

He grunted for me to move along and not in a
friendly, go back and get more way. No, this was a
clear message - you complain about the food, you
don't get any. He stared at me like he was
begging me to challenge him.

As much as I was not looking forward to a lunch of
brown slop, I was not happy about going hungry. I
felt my temper starting to get the better of me but
for once, I did the smart thing. Or close to the

smart thing. I winked at Rhino and said, "Guess no one can really take a joke around here, huh?" He stared at me like I was babbling nonsense, just like his buddy had in the food line. I moved on and at dinner I was hungry enough to be glad for our brown gloop. I guess that's the idea.

The next day when I saw Tiny become a pile of jello I was really glad I had kept my mouth shut. When I looked around the Yard that day, I counted a hundred prisoners and only ten Rhinos. Most of the prisoners looked away and didn't even watch what happened to Tiny. Like they were ashamed in some way. I wondered what would happen if we all turned on the Rhinos at once. Looking at those half-starved, beaten into submission prisoners staring at the ground, that seemed as unlikely as a rescue ship appearing for me out of nowhere. A fellow can dream, can't he?

Chapter 6

Alright. Back to Xaralien. And how I got off
Xaralien. And how I learned to fly a spaceship.
And how I ended up in the Yazoulian Outlands.
And brushed up against Dr. Z. And met Norman
Howard. And Lata (mmm Lata - I don't know
whether to cry or smile at her memory). As I
mentioned, Jack Lightsky warned me. He told me,
"Most guys do stupid things for pretty girls. Don't
let yourself be one of them." Did I listen? Well, we
all know the answer to that question. Well, maybe
you don't yet. But you will. And again I am getting
ahead of myself. I really need to stop doing that.

There I was on Xaralien. The Volchinks after me. I
had no money and no food. I hung around outside
the back door of some restaurants for a couple of

days and picked out food from the food they threw

away at the end of the night. I felt like a human

raccoon. I wasn't sure what would happen first -

me starving or getting caught by the Volchinks. I

had found an empty loft to sleep in so I had a roof

over my head. And I tried to only go out at night.

This went on for a couple of days that seemed like

a couple of years.

Down at the Spaceport dock, I found the lowliest worker in the place. A janitor who didn't seem to ever go anywhere without his mop-vacuum slung over his shoulder. On most spaceports, janitors are all robots. I figured this guy must be working for next to nothing to have beat out a robot for the job. Anyway, as I watched, no one ever spoke to the guy except to bark out an order to him of what to do next. I waited for his break and then went over and struck up a conversation. He looked startled at first like why would anyone talk to him? If he was suspicious, he didn't let on.

We were leaning against a building and standing in the shade to get out of the Red Sun. I made a little small talk about where he was from. Sonecto IV. He was surprised I knew anything about it. One of the Ice Planets with huge, Ice Bears that could eat a person in one bite. See, I was listening at least

some of the time in geography class.

He had ended up on Xaralien because he had

gone to work for one of the Union's official

smugglers. His name was Julie. Privateers, they

were called. They were given something called a

Mark by the Union. And that entitled them to

break the law and smuggle stolen goods around

the Universe. That made them Privateers instead of pirates.

I had never heard of such a thing. Legalized criminals! They didn't teach that in our Political Affairs class.

The Privateer had lost his Mark somehow. Julie thought it meant he didn't pay someone off. When they landed on Xaralien, the Volchinks arrested the guy and took his ship. Julie just slunk sway and took this job until he could figure out how to get off of Xarailen without having any money.

That's about when a group of Volchinks came walking by, not twenty yards from us. Luckily, they were yukking it up loudly so I heard them coming. I quickly turned my back to them and stepped into the shadows. Julie didn't say anything but I saw he noticed.

"What's the story with that guy with the mechanical arm and missing tooth? He doesn't seem to fit in around here?" I finally asked.

"That's Jack Lightsky. He's a Privateer just like my old boss. He has a Mark. I tried to get him to take me onto his crew but he said he doesn't need anyone right now. He's one of the last Privateers there is. They say they are doing away with them. Something about Dr. Z and Zoran but nobody really knows what those big muckety - mucks are up to." "You know, he continued, if you want to get off this planet, there's a way I could help you."

He looked at me and I thought I saw something in

his eyes. Just little flicker or a pause. Something I should have paid attention to but didn't. But always will from now on.

"There's a hatch into Lightsky's ship that you could fit into but I'm too big for or I would do it myself. I can sneak you into it tonight and he leaves tomorrow morning. He'll never know you're there. He's going to hit a Dark Seam and then you'll be a million miles from this place by the time he finds you're on board."

I hesitated but then I agreed. I guess I wanted off Xaralien so bad I couldn't think straight. I guess I wanted to believe this guy was so appreciative someone had stopped to notice him that he was willing to risk ending up in prison to help a total stranger. That's the last time I would be so easily fooled (at least until I met Lata).

So that night, I met Julie at the arranged time. He led me to the ship. We passed some private security guards but no Volchinks. Julie flashed his ID at them and they let us pass. The ship was dark and quiet. Julie told me in a whisper not to make a sound. He led me to a small hatch that I could just about squeeze into. No way he could have fit. I was thanking him for his help while I squirmed into the compartment when all of a sudden the dark and stillness was shattered.

A huge spotlight lit us and the ship up and out of the darkness stepped a dozen Volchinks. I looked at Julie and he actually smiled at me. "Sorry kid, they said they'd give me a reward. Then I can get off this planet. Nothing personal. Just business." My mouth opened but no words came out. Two Volchinks grabbed me roughly, each one gripping one of my arms. I felt so stupid for having trusted Julie, I couldn't even be mad at him. After all, can you get mad at a red-headed, giant venominator just because it acts like the snake it is? No, you just head away from it or you are stupid. And that was me - stupid.

As the Volchinks started to pull me down the plank of the ship, there was a commotion and Jack

Lightsky appeared. He was in his pajamas and some of his long hair was sticking up in strange directions. But at his side was a double phaser laser cannon that was illegal everywhere in the Union. "What are you doing on my ship?" His voice boomed. The Volchinks continued to pull me but something told me to resist for a minute to see how this played out. I wriggled out of their grip while they were looking at Jack. One of them reached for me. "You little rat, get over here," he said, trying to grab me again.

"Hold it right there," Jack's voice boomed again. This time, the laser cannon was pointed at the Volchinks.

"Watch what you're doing, pirate. You're pointing a weapon at an agent of the Union."

"You better think twice about that," the other Volchink said.

"And you're trespassing on the ship of a Privateer - not a Pirate - with a Mark issued by Zoran." Jack said. "I'm legally entitled to blow your head off right now. You're the one breaking the law. You aren't allowed on this ship without a written order from a Galaxy Governor presented to me in advance. I could shoot you or have you arrested. Which one would you like?"

The Volchinks' mouths tried to speak but no words came. Finally, one said, "Why do you care about this little runaway rat? If you won't let us take him, we'll just wait on the dock for you to throw him off your ship. And then we'll take him!"

I saw Julie's face brighten at this and I wanted to reach over and smack that smile off him. Lightsky looked at me and then at Julie and the Volchinks. "When I throw him off, you can do what you want. Until then get off or I start shooting."

My heart sank as I watched them assemble on the dock. How would I get past them when he threw me off. It was impossible.

Lightsky looked at me. "What's your name, kid?" I told him. "Okay, Terry," he said. "Welcome to my ship. I hope you don't mind hard work." "You mean you're not throwing me off?" I could barely get the words out.

"Throw you to the Volchinks? That is something Jack Lightsky would never do to another man. I'm a pirate, son. No matter what that piece of paper they gave me calls me. And no pirate turns someone in who is being chased by dirty Volchinks. Now get below and let's get ready to get out of here in the morning."

He put his hand on my shoulder and directed me below. And for the first time since I left Crystal Z, I felt like I was home.

And did I mention the color of Jack Lightsky's ship. The darkest shade of pitch black.

Chapter 7

And so began my great adventure with Jack Lightsky, the man with one mechanical arm. I didn't know why Jack helped me when Julie betrayed me. He said, "Kid, I don't know myself. I hate Volchinks, I guess. And I hate people telling me what to do."

"So, it really gets my blood going when a Volchink tells me what to do. I think I'm just a stubborn old guy that way."

We flew anywhere and everywhere in the Territories. That's the charted part of the Universe that does not belong to the Union or to one of the other 25 smaller planetary federations. Not exactly lawless but not exactly civilized and law abiding. We boarded ships with blasters drawn in one quadrant and then handed our stolen cargo off by telepathing across the Universe. Jack's ship had cloaking so it could fly through radars undetected. We would suddenly appear next to an unsuspecting ship, our laser cannons out and encircle them with an electronic field that disabled their ship weapons. Jack told me only Privateers had this type of technology. And of course, Volchink ships. Back then the Privateers were legal and Volchink ships didn't bother them.

Jack explained the difference between a Privateer and pirate and why the Volchinks backed off. "Because the Territories - which by the way are six galaxies wide - are not under the control of the Union, they aren't all that safe. But people still need all the same things - food, houses, games, clothes and so on. The ships that bring those things are sitting ducks for pirates. The pirates steal the cargos and sell them in the Union or one of the other Federations. This isn't great for the Union because they don't get any tax money then."

So, Zoran gave a few lucky pirates licenses to steal as long as they paid the Union. They were called Privateers and given something called a Mark to show who they were. They could come and go anywhere in the Union and no Volchink or tax man could do a thing about it. And the whole thing is secret. No one knows about it.

All Jack had to do was keep paying the Union. And stay out of the way of pirates, who hated the Privateers.

Jack told me stories of the pirates and the remote and desolate planets where they hid their plunder.

It was on one of those planets that he lost his arm in a battle with a rival band that had tracked him and his crew there. They attacked them as they were unloading their ship. That was before Jack became a Privateer. Now he unloads in spaceports just like any other cargo ship.

Did I tell you that the Volchinks hate the Privateers even more than the Privateers hate the Volchinks? They don't like the idea that there is anyone in the Union who isn't subject to their authority.

Especially people like Jack, who like to let them know that they can't touch them. After all, what's the point of being a low-down, scum of a Volchink if you can't boss everyone around and lock up whoever you feel like? Isn't that the whole point?

Now some would say Jack took me in and saved me out of the goodness of his heart. Me, I wasn't sure there was much goodness in there. After all, we stole ships filled with food that were going to places that needed it and sold it to food brokers in the Union for their wealthy clients. We stole shipments of spare parts that were intended to keep the power plants on ice planets going so people didn't freeze. If there was a profit to be made, we stole it.

Jack said, "Every man needs a Code. And you have to stick to that Code."

I told him, "steal anything , and everything" didn't seem like much of a Code to me. He looked at me with mean little eyes and raised that mechanical arm. I thought he was going to smack me with it and I flinched. But he just clapped me on the back with a friendly tap and smiled and laughed.

"Terry, you figured me out. My Code is take what you want and get what you can. It's a mean universe out there. No one is cutting the likes of us any breaks. I have just one rule - I try not to hurt anyone if I can help it." So, that was the extent of Jack's goodness - he wouldn't shoot you unless he had to. And some times, he did have to. And he seemed to have more than one rule but somehow they all came down to "look out for no. 1, no one else will."

Most cargo ships gave up without a fight. The crew wasn't interested in getting blasted so some corporate boss could get rich. But every now and then, someone - usually a young kid, all full of spunk - tried to stand up and stop us.

The problem was that laser blasters like Jack carried are not only illegal, they are almost impossible to get. So Jack had every cargo ship outgunned. The most they ever had was pellet guns. Jack called them "baby toys." I was standing next to him when one of the crew on a cargo ship of medical supplies went for a hidden pellet gun. One of the senior crew members had been begging, trying to convince us to leave the supplies be. That they were needed on the planet Gavallon at hospitals and people would die without them. I could see Jack was getting annoyed but I figured he would just ignore the guy - his Code and all. That was when the young guy on the other side of the room went for his pellet gun. I guess he thought Jack wasn't paying attention because he was listening to the other guy. He was wrong. Jack zapped him with his laser without a second thought or a blink of an eye.

No, goodness in his heart was in short supply. I figured Jack saw me as good cheap labor. He taught me to fly his ship and the pay was right - for

him. He gave me food and a place that was safe

from the Volchinks. Occasionally he threw me a

few digits. Considering that the hardest and most

expensive thing for a Privateer to find are crew

members who have any brains and can be trusted

he was making out big time with me. Jack saw

that I had brains. And he knew I had nowhere to

go so I could be trusted. And the price was right.

Pretty much room and board where his usual crew

would want a share of the spoils and then might

even try and steal the rest. It was a sweet deal -

for Jack. Not that I'm complaining.

And it turned out I was a pretty great pilot. Must

have been all the time I wasted playing video

games instead of studying. I took right to it. And

soon I was better than Jack. I could operate those

controls with my eyes closed. The dials and knobs and buttons seemed to be imprinted in my brain. I could out run pirate ships, dodge the fastest air patrols, navigate through meteor showers and gas clouds, hide from search parties behind moons at night - you name it - if it involved that ship - I could do it.

I thought of all the things the ship could do, cloaking was the coolest. That was where the ship could become invisible. The only ships in the Universe that have that belong to the Volchinks and maybe Zoran's personal fleet. Jack would never tell me how he got it. He would just smile and say he might tell me "someday."

The only problem with cloaking was that you could only use it once a day for up to an hour. Then the mechanism needed to recharge.

One time in the Ravashon planetary belt, we were hiding from some Ravashon Space Rangers with a cargo of minerals to get to a shipping colony in the Outland Federation. We were cloaked for too long and I knew we were going to light up any minute. We were sitting right in the middle of the Ranger patrol. We would be sitting ducks once the cloak wore off.

I was sweating that they would bump into us but I knew anytime now they would see us, bright as a shiny star. But just before our cloaking turned off,

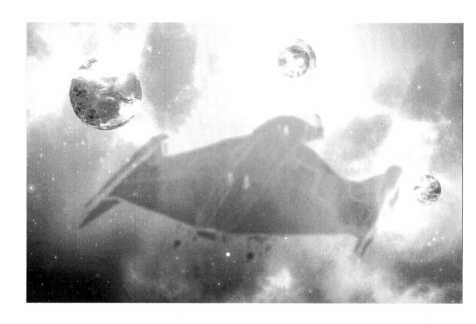

they moved on. When I looked down at the ship controls I saw they were a little wet. I wondered if we had a leak somewhere but then realized it was from my sweat. I had been so nervous, I was covered in sweat. Jack laughed at me over that one.

"Never let them see you sweat, kid" he told me. "The guys who get away are the ones who don't get nervous. Next time you're in a tight spot, instead of getting nervous, just picture how you are going to get out of it and focus on that. Then try and stay calm and make it happen."

Did I mention Jack loved to offer little pearls of advice like that? The thing is, a lot of them made sense. Even today when I'm in a tight spot, I find myself thinking, now what would Jack do?

I had fun with Jack. I wondered if I should feel bad about some of the things we did. I was still grateful though - after all, he did save me from the

Volchinks. But I paid him back a thousand times -
as even he admitted. As he said, "Who would
have thought that picking up some scrawny kid on
some planet in the middle of nowhere would be
the best investment I ever made?" Then he would
laugh. But I knew he meant every word. I could
swear I saw his eyes lighting up at all the money I
had saved him and made him.

Jack saved me. And taught me to fly. And gave
me lots of advice I still remember. And took me all
over the Universe. But not from goodness. That
wasn't part of his Code.

Chapter 8

After the Rhino guards zapped Tiny in the Yard,
they decided that wasn't enough punishment for
him. They wanted to make an example of him. So
they kept picking on him. They would knock his
food tray over and make him clean it up. They
would come into his room in the middle of the
night and wake him up for a security check and
make him stand up for an hour while they

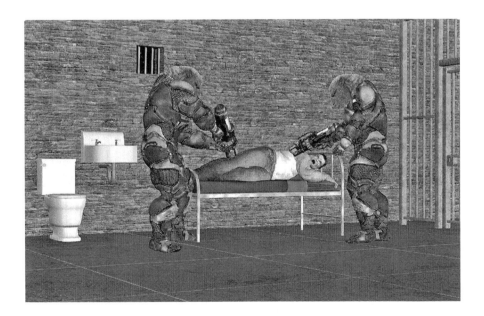

searched his little postcard room over and over for an hour.

They would come up to him in line and tell him he had stepped out of line and had to go to the end of the line. When it was time to go into the Yard - the only chance we ever got to go outside - they would sometimes call his name and tell him he was wanted in the office. He would shuffle off with two of the guards only to find each time that it was a mistake - no one had called for him. By the time he got back, Yard time would be over.

Since I had helped him that day in the Yard, we had become kind of friends. I couldn't do much to help when the Rhinos picked on him. A couple of times I was right next to him when they did these things. One time when they told him he had stepped out of line for the bathroom (after we had waited a half hour and were just about to go in), I tensed up and started to protest that he had done no such thing. Tiny grabbed my arm and whispered, "That's okay, kid. You don't need any trouble." And off he shuffled to the end of the line to wait another half an hour.

One time when they knocked his tray over, I turned to look at the Rhino who had done it. His eyes were dead as if he didn't even see me. He had a red dot on his forehead. I stared into those dead Rhino eyes and I felt like fire was coming out of my eyes. My whole body seemed to rise up and I gripped my tray so hard I thought it would break.

Tiny was smarter than me though. He just bent over and started to clean up the food from the floor. He mumbled, "Not now, kid, not now."

I'm not proud to say I backed off without doing anything but I remembered that red dot.

I did manage to laugh and smile and say "Tiny, you are so clumsy. You got to stop dropping your tray like that. If you don't want your food, just throw it away next time."

Then I looked at red dot with as dumb a smile on my face as I could put there.
His dead eyes didn't even blink. If he heard anything I said, I couldn't tell.

Tiny explained to me how Prestis 3 really worked. None of the prisoners stayed there for long. They could either buy their way out or be shipped off to do twenty years hard labor on a planet in the

Mineral Belt. I guess the companies that owned the mines like prisoner workers. The price is certainly right.

Tiny knew he was going on the next ship, which would be on Prestis in a few weeks. He didn't have any money or anyone who could pay off the Warden. I told him I hadn't even had a trial yet and I was technically a minor. I shouldn't even be eligible for a prison sentence. I should be sent to some camp for bad kids or something. Tiny laughed at that one.

"Kid," he said, "the only trial here is can you pay your way out of here. If you can't you're going to a mineral planet."

I thought about the computer disk at the

Spacetrain station. I thought about my ship. At the Spaceport, I hoped. Either one was valuable but didn't seem to do me any good. The disk might be worth something to Dr. Z but if I said that, all I would get was a laugh. And how could I trade the ship? I doubted it was still there. Lata probably had it on the other side of the galaxy by now.

It happened that Tiny and I worked in the prison laundry together. That was where we were when my name (the fake one I had given anyway) was

called over the loudspeaker. Two Rhinos appeared out of nowhere and grunted at me to follow them. I asked them what this was about but they just stared at me like I was babbling nonsense.

The prison laundry was on the fifth floor of the prison. There were bars on all of the windows but you could see outside. Once a week I would watch the big laundry truck as it pulled up to the prison empty. Then the Rhinos would fill it up with stacks of sheets and pillows and pillowcases and blankets. Then it would pull away and the guards would wave it right through the gate. I didn't understand why the clean new-looking laundry supplies were leaving the prison and we were sweating in the laundry room cleaning old soiled sheets that had been around forever. I just wanted to get from that fifth floor to that truck. But with those bars on the windows, that was impossible.

There was a laundry chute where we sent the clean (or what passed for clean) laundry but that chute went only to a basement where the Rhino guards took care of whatever was sent down the chute. I thought about going down the chute and popping out - "Surprise," I would yell. Then what would I do after they took turns zapping me? Well, a fellow can dream, can't he?

That day, after my fake name was called and the Rhinos came for me, we went through the prison to the Warden's office. They brought me inside and told me (or more like grunted with a nod of their Rhino heads towards the chair) to sit down.

Then in came the Warden. I had never met him

before. He sat down behind his desk and smiled

at me. It was a pretty phony, oily kind of smile. In

fact, he was a pretty oily kind of guy. Beady little

eyes, a little rabbit nose, a sweaty forehead and

greasy black hair, slicked back. He was short too.

I could see he was wearing an expensive suit

though. And he had a fancy gold watch - Quarlex,

I believe. Jack and I once lifted a shipment of

those from a transport. Those babies are very

expensive. I thought only the super-rich could afford them. That was one of our luckiest- and best paying - jobs ever. How could a prison warden afford a suit like that and a Quarlex?

Well, I didn't have much time to wonder about it as the Warden looked at me and the first thing he said took me by surprise. "Terence Moor-Yamalon", he said looking down at some papers. "Last seen three years ago on Xaralien. Seems like the Volchinks have been looking for you for a while."

I wondered how he got my real name but then I remembered the DNA swab they took on my first day. I actually perked up at the thought of being sent back to Xaralien instead of a prison mine. I would worry about my ship and the disk once I got out of here.

"But sorry to say, they don't want you. Or at least they don't want you enough to pay 500 digits for you. So, this is your chance - actually your last chance." He stared those beady eyes at me. "If there is anyone out there who will pay 500 digits, that's what it will cost to keep you from being shipped off to a prison mine."

Now, I have a price on my head, you might remember - 20,000 digits. But that's not for Terry - only Black Shadow. And no one knows I'm Black Shadow. And Black Shadow has already been sentenced to life in a space pod by Zoran for what happened to Norman Howard (not my fault, but who's going to believe me?) So, I didn't see that telling the Warden I'm Black Shadow would help matters, even if he believed me.

That was when I noticed the folders on his desk. JVH laundry, one said. Another said JVH Food. A third, JVH Transport. It all clicked. The dirty sheets, the crummy food, the trucks leaving filled with brand new supplies. The fancy suit and expensive watch. The Warden was a thief. He was stealing and selling supplies.

I just looked at him and his sweaty forehead. "How's the laundry business?" was all I said. He stared at me and I could see, first surprise, then hate. "You should have stayed on Xaralien" was all he said. Or more like snorted. "The next mineral transport is next week. You'll be on it. Good luck." He nodded at the guards and they led me out. I could see him quickly shoving the folders into his desk drawer.

When I told Tiny we had one week to figure

something out, he just shook his head. He said,

"There's nothing we can do, Terry. We're done for."

I felt sorry for him, he seemed so sad. Even

though I was in the same boat as him.

I tried to remember what Jack had told me about

being in a tight spot. "Picture the way out, stay

calm and make it happen."

I tried but for the life of me, I couldn't picture the

way out, let alone figure out how to make it

happen.

Chapter 9

I think I mentioned that the Yazoulian Outlands

was important to my story. And that I would get to

it later. Well, no time like the present. I think I also

mentioned that once upon a time when I was a

little 5 year old, I actually had parents. And that I

was snatched away from them like all the other

Intells just because I did well on a test. And that I

would tell you the worst part of that story. Well,

get ready. It isn't pretty.

I know I haven't mentioned my parents much but I do remember them. I also remember being pretty happy with them, like most 5 year olds. They loved me, I loved them. I didn't listen. They yelled at me. I had a temper tantrum. They took my toys away. I yelled at them some more. They yelled at me. We made up. You know - the usual. I wasn't the easiest 5 year old but I was theirs and they were mine. My Dad had an ordinary job in an office for some big company. I don't know what he did or what the company did. After all, I was only 5. I do remember that I was from the planet Crystal -Z. In the back of my mind, I was determined to get back there. The whole time Jack and I were flying around the Universe (I know - the Known Universe), I kept my eye out for if we ever got anywhere near Crystal -Z. But Crystal -Z was part of the Union. We never had any reason to go anywhere near there. Our territory was the fringes and outliers, some semi-civilized and some completely lawless. Occasionally, we touched down on a Union outpost like when I met Jack on Xaralien. But those were border planets where we quickly sold our cargoes and then headed back out.

After a couple of years of flying with Jack and a lot of adventures and a lot of money made- for Jack, not me - two important things happened. They were connected - or at least they became connected (is that a thing?) - but I didn't realize it at the time.

The first was Jack got a message about a big job on Vegastopia 23. It was a pick up of a valuable but small package. Jack said it could be our biggest score ever. His eyes really lit up when he said that. He even smacked his lips and I could swear I saw a little drool. I had never seen him so excited. "Pick up might be the wrong word, kid. More like a pick-off, if you know what I mean." He laughed that big loud laugh of his. "But it should be like taking candy from a baby. As easy as pie."

So, off we went towards Vegastopia. Which so you have your bearings is in the Territories right over the border from the Yazoulian Outlands, which is the farthest galaxy of the Union. On the other side of the Outlands is the Mineral Belt. The planets of the Outlands are the most desolate and unpleasant places in the Union. They include all the Union prisons (like on Prestis 1, 2, and 3) and a lot of military bases and a bunch of planets where no one knows much of anything that goes on.

So we touched down on Yazoo -1 in the Outlands on our way to Vegastopia. Jack still wouldn't tell me what the job was about. But I think he chose Yazoo -1 to refuel for a reason. See, I had told Jack my story about being snatched from my parents. I filled him in as we flew through the solar systems on all the creeps I had been subjected to - Alberto and all the rest - and I usually got pretty worked up telling it. Jack would just laugh and say "Keep fighting, kid. Don't ever give up. That's what I like about you. Stay mad. Don't ever stop fighting."

I always thought he wasn't listening and was just blowing me off. I guess I was wrong.

From the minute we left our ship on Yazoo -1, the place creeped me out. It looked nice enough from the ship. Modern, gleaming buildings everywhere with plenty of green spaces. Not what you would expect from an Outland planet.

But the people - if you can call them that - that is what made the place so creepy. They looked normal enough, just like everyday humans. But there was something strange about the look in their eyes. From the first guys who met the ship and directed us to the space dock to the customs woman who took our papers and stamped them.

There was something off. Something missing, like they saw us but looked right through us. They looked us up and down like they were registering or scanning us. It was weird when the first guy did it but it was weirder when everyone did it. And their voices. They were normal human voices but they were all so polite and spoke with perfect grammar.

Transport drivers are usually smelly like they just had an onion and garlic sandwich and look and smell like they haven't bathed for a few days. Not on Yazoo -1. There they sound like they might be a Professor teaching classical literature at the Sorbonnic Harvasian Institue in Oxfordville. We got out at a large white building with a sign that said Ministry of Records.

"What's up with this place," I asked Jack. "And what are we doing here?" I pointed to the building.

"Kid," Jack said, "Yazoo -1 is the robot-person planet. Everyone in the Union thinks putting chips in peoples brains is outlawed. But everyone here has a chip in their brain. And there's something else. The people who are sent here and given the chips -they are the parents of the Intells." "What?" I stammered and actually felt my knees buckle. Jack grabbed my arm and held me up so I didn't fall.

"That's right, kid," Jack said. "So all the parents don't make trouble about their missing kids, they swoop them up and bring them here. Implant a chip and put them to work. Instead of a bunch of unhappy parents, the Union gets super smart workers who probably can't even remember their kids."

"Can't remember?" I was trying to stay calm but it wasn't working. I felt sweaty and sick. I looked up at the white Ministry building. "And what's this?" was all I could manage.

"This is where they keep the records. They can tell you where your parents are. If you want to know."

"Of course I want to know," I said. "Will they just tell me?"

"No, they won't just tell you but I have a friend here and for a few digits, he will get us the info." Jack said.

"How many digits?" My pockets were not exactly overflowing from Jack's generosity.

"Kid - it's on me." Jack said, and I have to say I was surprised. Occasionally Jack could really surprise you. "If you really want to know. Are you sure?"

"Of course I'm sure," I said although I was far

from sure.

"Wait here then." And Jack turned and went up the steps and into the white Ministry building. I watched him get smaller and smaller as he went up the steps and there were a lot steps - and I felt as he walked my dream of going back to Crystal - Z and my parents were getting smaller and smaller with him.

So, to make a long story short, as they say, Jack got the info. We hopped into a Transport and crossed halfway across the planet. My parents lived in a beautiful house with a large garden. They had two little kids. They walked around with smiles and the same blank eyes as everyone else on the planet and spoke in the same calm, peaceful voices with the same perfect grammar. And they didn't remember me at all. Not a flicker of recognition in their robot chip brains.

And yes, I felt a little like my guts had been ripped out of me. All the years floating and fighting from one place to another across the galaxies, I at least thought there was somewhere I actually belonged. Now I knew I belonged nowhere. I was totally like those pieces of space junk floating aimlessly that we ducked in our ship. They had no home and were going nowhere - just like me. It was an eerie feeling. Was Jack now all I had?

I think Jack felt bad for me. He tried to cheer me up. He talked about the big job we had coming up on Vegastopia. And how we could take a few days there before and relax and have some fun. He said you haven't seen girls until you've seen the girls on Vegastopia. He even promised me a piece of the action from the big job. I figured he must really feel bad for me because Jack never promised me anything. But there was something about the way he talked about this job. He seemed nervous somehow. And Jack Lightsky was never nervous - or at least I had never seen him nervous. When I asked him about it, he laughed and told me it was my imagination.

"I told you kid," he said. "This job will be like taking candy from a baby. Nothing to it."

And so off we went to Vegastopia 23. The home planet of Dr. Z and Blizzard and Crusher and Vankenson and the entire Dark Justice crew. Babies? Not exactly. Not at all.

Chapter 10

Now the next part of my story, you may be scratching your head and asking how do I know all this? I wasn't there so how can I be telling you what happened? Well, all I can say is that I pieced it together from what I know and what I was told. And if I got a few details wrong, well, I'm sure I got most of it pretty close to right.

Remember I told you about the scientists working on Hobotian on an improved teletransport device. Basically, it was a bunch of creepy Humanoids with two human guys in charge. Zoran apparently felt that if a human like Dr. Z invented the best teletransport, then he Zoran needed a human in charge. And being Zoran, he decided two is always better than one so he put two humans in charge. Mr. no 2 was Norman Howard and his boss was a guy named Jonathan Sires. Norman Howard was a really smart guy - maybe not Dr. Z - who is? - but still a genius. At science that is, not at everything else, as you'll see. Jonathan Sires may have been smart but he was no genius. He wasn't even a scientist. He was a military guy who Zoran trusted. One big problem: he was mean and nasty through and through to the tiniest bone in his body. Like I said, what is it about mean guys in charge?

Sires loved to mistreat Norman Howard. Maybe because he was the only other real human around. He could mistreat the Humanoids all he wanted but they wouldn't care, probably wouldn't even know and would never react. So, that left only poor Norman. And mistreat him he did. He picked on the poor guy and bullied him in all kinds of ways.

There were small ways like asking him to run

downstairs for papers Jonathan Sires already had.

Only to discover them before Norman returned.

Having him redo reports over and over that Sires

didn't even understand because he said the

grammar was incorrect in a sentence or two. Even

making him run out for coffee even though there

were plenty of Humanoids to do it. One of Sires

favorites was to send Norman to the factory - a full

hour away - at the end of the day to get something Sires needed urgently. When Norman returned, hours later, Sires would be nowhere in sight, having gone home for the night. Worse of all, Sires berated Norman constantly over their lack of progress. Or what Sires considered lack of progress.

Since Sires wasn't a scientist, he had no idea if they were making progress. All he knew was that when he asked Norman if they had the device yet, the answer was always no. When he asked if they were close, the answer was always, we're making progress.

This went on for two years. And as time passed, Sires got meaner and meaner. Zoran wanted progress and Sires wasn't delivering. Which meant Norman Howard wasn't delivering.

Meanwhile, Norman's fellow scientist Dr. Z was

basically the richest guy in the Universe. You can

see how all of that might bother Norman.

What makes these scientist guys snap? Being

picked on their whole lives? Being pushed around

by people way dumber than they are? Who

knows. But Norman snapped, big-time. If

snapping means deciding to go off on your own

and double-cross Zoran and get rich. I guess

some people would just call that coming to your

senses.

As you can imagine, the security on Hobotian was

pretty, well, secure. Being as how they were

working on the most top-secret project in the

Universe on a planet run by an ex-soldier. Nothing

got on or off Hobotian without being inspected down to the last molecule. Jonathan Sires might not know much about science but he knew security.

In the category of things he didn't know were three pretty big ones about Norman Howard. First, he was a lot closer to solving the tele transport problem than he had let on. Second, he had taught himself to fly a space ship. And third - and this is big and a little complicated - he had invented another pretty neat device. It was a freeze or stop-motion jiggy. Don't ask me how but with the press of a button all human activity within a mile froze for something like fifteen minutes. Best of all he had a little zapper thing-a-majiggy that went with it where he could zap someone and they - and only they - would unfreeze while everyone else stayed frozen. Pretty crazy, I know.

Amazing what these genius guys can come up with.

If I could invent stuff like that, I wouldn't want someone like Sires sending me for coffee or yelling at me all the time either. Actually, I wouldn't want to put up with those things even though I can't invent things. Well, I hope Sires got what was coming to him because I'm sure you can see where this is going.

One day - just before we visited Yazoulian -

Norman Howard picked himself up, grabbed a computer disk with his teletransport work on it and went down to the Hobotian space shuttle station. When the first guard asked him for a pass, he took his little freezer out and pressed the button at the same time he zapped himself. Everyone in the shuttle station was immediately frozen but only for fifteen minutes. He hurried to a space cruiser, fired it up and took off. Setting a course for Vegastopia 23. The one place where he knew there was someone who would pay a fortune for what was on that disk - Dr. Z.

The only problem was that Norman Howard wasn't really the criminal type even though he had just committed one of the biggest crimes in history. How do I figure that? Well, if you figure how much teletransport is worth - it must be billions. And that's what he stole from Zoran. Which hopefully got him mad enough to take it out on Jonathan Sires.

But back to Vegastopia and Norman Howard. He checked into a nice hotel but since he knew Vegastopia was off-limits to Zoran and Volchinks he used his real name. I know - for a smart guy - not smart. Of course, Zoran had every agent in the Union looking for Norman. So, it only took a half hour or maybe an hour for Zoran and the Volchinks to know where Norman was. And that's where Jack and I come into the story. Since

Volchinks or anyone else working for Zoran can't operate on Vegastopia, the Union needed someone to get that disk who didn't work for Zoran. Someone who would deliver it to the Volchinks. Someone like a Privateer whose livelihood depended on being in Zoran's good graces. Someone smart and tough. Someone like Jack Lightsky.

Unfortunately for everyone - especially me - someone got in the way. That's right. You guessed it. Lata.

Chapter 11

Meanwhile, back on Prestis 3, the Rhinos were just

as ugly, their breath still stank and the food didn't

resemble anything you would want to eat. In other

words, same old, same old. They did seem to

have given up picking on Tiny. I was thinking that

wasn't really a good sign. It was kind of like they

knew we were being shipped off to work (die?) in

the mines and were taking Rhino pity on us. Is

that possible? Is there such a thing?

I knew that time was getting short for me and Tiny.

The rumor was we were down to six days. It

turned out we had almost two weeks. I know -

whoopee. But we didn't know that. I kept trying

the Lightsky method - picturing my way out but

the picture was blank. As I walked through the

Yard each day, I looked all around, hoping something would stir my imagination as a possible way out. But nothing.

I watched every day as the laundry delivery truck loaded up and went through the gates. But it loaded at the bottom of the laundry chute and there were guards at the top and guards at the bottom. So there was no way to get into the bales of laundry (or should I call it stolen supplies padding the Warden's pockets - boy that burned me up). Which was too bad because the guards at the gate didn't check the back of the truck. I watched as they just waved it through. Anyone hiding under the supplies would be waved through without anyone knowing. It just didn't seem possible to get into the truck since it was surrounded by guards the whole time it was loading.

As I watched it on the morning of what I called Day 6, I sighed. What was I missing? Then I saw it. As bright and clear as if Jack Lightsky had been there himself. As the truck made the turn toward the gate, no one was really paying attention any more. The guards who supervised the loading had all turned away and were going off in different directions, chatting and snorting Rhino at each other. But there was a moment. Maybe just an instant - when the truck passed by one of the buildings - an electrical shed that was three stories high with a slanted roof. In that instant, someone on that roof could jump and if they landed on the bales of laundry supplies, they could probably cushion the impact. If they missed - well then, it would be all over and the Rhinos would be scraping them up like flattened pancakes.

The one thing - and it wasn't exactly a teeny

weeny thing - was how to get onto that roof at

precisely the moment when the truck is passing

by. How to get on there at all, let alone at the

exact right time? I spent pretty much all of Day 6

staring across the Yard at the shed. I pictured me

and Tiny climbing up the side of the building like

spiders or jumping from building roof to building

roof. Of course, if we could have done those

things, we would have been able to escape long

ago.

Day 5 I spent staring at the door to the shed instead of the roof. If we couldn't go directly to the roof, the only other way was to go in the front door and go up the steps. That easy, right? What would make the Rhinos open up that door? And how could we be there at the exact moment they did so? I thought about that all through Day 5. I was trying hard to stay calm like Jack would have wanted but it was getting harder and harder to do. In my mind I could hear the doors of the transport ship slamming shut and my stomach knotted and my hands got clammy. I knew that wouldn't help me though. I had to concentrate and block everything else out, except that shed.

It was the very end of Day 5 that it hit me. It wasn't perfect. Far from it. But it was a plan. It was hope. It was a chance. It came to me standing in line at the Rhino gruel cafe for lunch. I looked down at the utensils in my hand. They were made of landrium. A lightweight material that resembled plastic but was not plastic so it was washable and something like metal. But unlike metal utensils landrium ones could not hurt anyone. If you tried to stab someone with landrium it would bend like rubber. I remembered geography class again. When discovered on one of the Mineral Belt planets, landrium set off a modern day gold rush that made a lot of people very rich. It also had another very unusual property, known to very few people. Something mentioned in passing at Liberty Shades that I remembered only because all the stories about the Mineral Planets interested me even when I wasn't paying attention.   It was a super conductor of electricity. As I scooped my gruel with my landrium fork, the pieces of my plan fell into place.

Day 4 I spent filling Tiny in on the plan. I could tell he wasn't really buying it even though he really wanted to. He knew what was going to happen to us if this didn't work. He wanted to believe it could get us out. "How come no one else has ever done this" he asked.

It was the right question. A good question. One I had no answer for. I wasn't sure I wanted him to know that though. So, I smiled and shrugged. "We are either the smartest guys that have ever been in here or the dumbest. I guess we'll find out."

That either satisfied him or scared him. But he stopped asking and said he was in. Of course, what choice did he have?

Day 3 we spent going over and over the plan. I had to admit it needed about a hundred things - okay maybe just 5 or 6 - but 5 or 6 big ones - to go exactly right. Just in case something stopped us from going forward, we planned on going forward on Day 2. That way we would have one more chance on Day 1 if something happened and interfered. Day 2 came and I had to admit I was nervous. I tried all the tricks Jack Lightsky taught me but none of them got rid of the butterflies in my stomach. I looked at Tiny. His face was like stone. He either was determined or resigned that we were headed for disaster. I couldn't tell which and I didn't want to know.

The laundry truck would be leaving at 3:00, the same as every other day. By then shadows would be coming off the buildings. At 2:30 I slapped

Tiny's thigh and said, "It's go time." He nodded and we separated in the big prison Yard.

2:40: Step one. I took a landrium spoon I had smuggled out of the lunchroom into the prison library, where I was conveniently volunteering that week. I went over to one of the computers set up for the inmates that was not in use. I took the landrium spoon and jammed it into the electrical outlet where the computer was plugged in. The outlet seemed to sizzle and blink red and I left the library. As I passed a Rhino guard on my way back to the Yard, I saw lights flicker and go dark in a section of the library. As I went outside I looked at the electrical shed. I couldn't see Tiny and hoped that meant he was there but well hidden.

Step two depended on a maintenance man

showing up without any Rhino guards. If they came with him, we were finished. What if no one came? What if they didn't come until the truck had left? I knew the answers to those questions and they weren't pretty.

2:45: I could feel the knot in my stomach release and unwind when a skinny maintenance man carrying a lunchpail of tools arrived at the shed. Alone. The second he unlocked the door and turned the doorknob and started to push it open,

there was a blur as Tiny came from nowhere. He pushed the maintenance guy through the door and slammed it shut. I smiled. For a big guy he moved awfully fast.

2:50: I entered the unlocked shed, making sure no Rhinos were watching. I found Tiny standing over a tied up maintenance man with masking tape over his mouth. He looked scared. Which was exactly how I felt. I locked the door and nodded at Tiny. He nodded back and we headed up the stairs to the roof.

2:55: We crawled onto the roof hoping none of the Rhinos in the guard towers could spot us. We crouched low and tried to stay in the shadows. I looked across the Yard and saw them as they finished loading the laundry truck. I took a deep breath and winked at Tiny. He wasn't fooled. He knew this was crazy. He didn't smile back.

3:00: The truck pulled out and headed towards us. We inched over towards the edge of the roof over where the truck would turn the corner. And for an instant be out of the view of the guards. For an instant.

3:02: I gripped Tiny's arm as the truck turned the corner. "Now," I whispered and jumped. I smashed into the soft bales of laundry and cushioned my head with my arm. I just hoped Tiny didn't fall on me. A second later I heard a loud thud. I looked over and saw Tiny. He gave me a thumbs up. We buried ourselves in the laundry, leaving openings so we could breathe.

3:05: The truck approached the gate. I held my breath as the truck slowed at the closed gate. If they looked at all, we were finished.

3:06: I heard some Rhino grunts and the truck started up again. Slowly at first then gaining speed. I smiled at Tiny. I wanted to yell or cry I was so happy. We had made it. We had done the impossible. Tiny was grinning like I had never seen before. I felt like a giant weight had just been lifted off me. We still had a lot to do to get off this planet but the hardest part was over. I actually felt myself start to relax - just a little.

3:15: The truck started to slow. Were we in town already? The truck came to a stop. We heard Rhino grunts. I looked at Tiny. He was as worried as me. This wasn't good. We could hear the

Rhinos getting closer. We heard them as they started moving the bales of laundry. I closed my eyes. Maybe they wouldn't get to us.

3:17: They pulled away the bales we were hiding under, exposing us. I looked up and standing there with the Rhinos was the slimy Warden. He smiled at me and I so much wanted to smack his oily face. I knew that wouldn't get me anywhere.

So I looked up and gave him my biggest smile.
"Nice day for a drive, isn't it?" I said as the Rhinos
grabbed us off the truck.

He gave me a little smile back. All he said was,
"Tomorrow." I knew what he meant.

Chapter 12

By now, you must be wondering if I am ever going to answer all those questions I have been putting off. Who is Lata? How did we meet? What did she have to do with Norman Howard? What happened between Jack and Norman Howard? Jack and Dr. Z? Dr. Z and me? How did I get the name Black Shadow? Why is there a reward for me? Where is my ship?

Whew. There are actually a lot more questions than I remembered. Well, no time like the present to start answering them. But pay attention because a lot is going to happen very fast.

First of all, Lata and Norman Howard. Now for a
super smart (did I hear anyone say genius) guy
Norman Howard was not so smart (does that make
sense?) When he got to Vegastopia 23 he asked
around for where he might be able to find some
criminal types. He ended up at a place called the
Black Rose. So far so good because the Black
Rose was a hangout for crooks, grifters, drifters
and broken down gangsters. In other words, every
type of anti-social individual looking to take

advantage of a nice, unsuspecting innocent non-criminal type. And even though he had just pulled off the biggest crime of the century (maybe of all time) Norman Howard was definitely the non-criminal type.

When he came into the Black Rose, he stuck out - can I say it - like a rose in a bed of thorns? No, too corny but you get the idea. And when he started asking about how he might meet Dr. Z, everyone who heard him laughed. The bartender shook his head in disbelief. How any of the run down losers in the Black Rose would ever know Dr. Z, probably the second most powerful person in the Known Universe - well, the idea is kind of funny. But one person seemed to take it seriously. That's right - Lata.

She came over and sat down next to Norman. And looked at him with those sparkling green eyes. And tossed that long red hair, like a swirl of fire. She leaned close so he could smell her perfume. By now, he was dizzy and lightheaded and confused about what he was doing there. She gently touched his knee and asked him "Why do you want to meet Dr. Z," as if it was the most normal thing in the world.

"Do you know him? I have something he would be very interested in." Norman Howard told her, trying hard to concentrate on his plan, not on her eyes.

"Of course I know him silly." She touched his knee again gently with two fingers, sending an electric spark that caused his face to flush. "Tell me more." She leaned in closer to his flushed face and when she shook her long red hair his body seemed to shake also.

So Norman Howard proceeded to tell Lata his story. The whole story from start to finish. Now you might ask how could such a smart guy be so dumb? Well, I'll take you back to the advice Jack Lightsky gave me - guys do stupid things for pretty girls. I can add to that - super smart guys do incredibly stupid things for pretty girls.

Well, Lata assured Norman Howard she could arrange the deal with Dr. Z. For her part, all she wanted from the whole thing was for Norman to pay her whatever he thought was "fair" once he was fabulously wealthy. And maybe they could go to a vacation planet for a few days to get to know each other. She leaned in closer when she said that and Norman might have handed over the disk right then if she had asked.

She told Norman not to talk to anyone else because he could not trust anyone. Except her, of course. He told her where he was staying and she told him especially not to tell anyone else that. She didn't even consider that he had used his real name and real identification for his hotel room.

Lata told him she would work on making the deal and meet him later. She kissed his cheek and he got even dizzier from her perfume. "Go back to your hotel room and wait for me. Don't go out and don't talk to anyone," she said to him as she left.

He nodded and did as he was told. He went back to his hotel and ordered room service. He felt incredibly lucky. The whole thing seemed like a dream. It was working out even better than he had ever expected. Not only was he about to be very rich but Lata also! He found himself thinking more about her than the money.

As you might suspect, Lata did not know Dr. Z. Sure, she had seen him at the Cyborg games sitting in his box overlooking the action. From the cheap seats where she sat, she could only see him with binocular glasses. He always seemed to have the same guys with him. Like everyone else on Vegastopia, she knew their names: Blizzard, Crystal, Vankenson, Crusher and Kittes. Lata also knew the club where Kittes, all 5 feet 5 with his little cat-like face, went after the Cyborg games. It was called Sinful. Kittes sat in a VIP area above the floor like Dr. Z at the Cyborg games (what is it with these guys - they think the higher up they sit, the more important they are?) He was always surrounded by bodyguards and the area was roped off. But Lata wasn't going to let that stop her.

She put on a sparkling blue dress and whispered in the doorman's ear at Sinful. He laughed and opened the door and waved off the cover charge.

Lata approached the roped-off VIP area and made eye contact with Kittes. As his bodyguards started to tell her this was a private area, Kittes waved them away and told them to let her pass.

She proceeded to work her charms on Kittes. Just like she had done with Norman Howard. Tossing her hair, leaning close, touching his knee. All her

tricks. Kittes smiled his cat-like smile with tiny,
pointy white teeth. Lata thought she was very
clever to let Kittes know what she had for sale
without telling him Norman Howard's name or
where to find him. While they were talking, Kittes
called one of his guards over. He whispered in the
man's ear and the man hurried off. Kittes and Lata
continued talking. He stared into her eyes just like
Norman Howard had but Kittes' face was blank
and his eyes were cold. The guard returned and
whispered in Kittes' ear and he nodded and the
guard left. Kittes returned his attention to Lata,
leaning closer than before. She really thought her
bag of tricks was working on him.

Poor Lata. For all her street smarts, she had no
idea who she was dealing with. Kittes agreed to
talk to Dr. Z and get back to her with a price. And

then they would arrange where and when to meet for the transfer. Lata hurried off to tell Norman Howard. She made sure she wasn't followed by looping in circles, going through crowded stores and doubling back a few times. Kittes would have laughed if he had seen her precautions. He didn't need to follow her.

One of Dr. Z's and Dark Justice's rules was never pay for something you can get for free. I imagine that rule especially applies when someone is trying to sell you stolen technology for tens of millions.

Lata hadn't told Kittes Norman Howard's name. But he didn't need her to tell him. Dr. Z and Kittes already knew Norman Howard's name and that he had stolen the technology he had been working on for Zoran. Now, thanks to Lata they knew he was on Vegastopia. And thanks to a quick data base search, done while the two of them talked, Kittes knew exactly where Norman Howard was staying. Since he had so conveniently used his real name at the hotel.

The first thing Kittes did when Lata left was call Vankenson who in turn went and had a quick word with Dr. Z. Then Vankenson called Kittes back and grabbed Blizzard to go pick Kittes up. They planned to pay a little social call on Norman Howard.

Meanwhile, in case you have forgotten Jack and I were also on Vegastopia. We had just arrived and Jack was still talking about "taking candy from a baby." He also was talking about how this was going to be his (I don't think he said our - I would remember that) big score. After this, the great

Jack Lightsky could finally hang it up and stop

chasing around the galaxies. He clapped his good

hand on my back. This would be the "big one" he

had been waiting for years to get. I wasn't sure

what my part in all of this was but I was pretty sure

Jack didn't see it as my chance for the big one.

Like I said, Jack was all about Jack.

We knew where Norman Howard was staying from the same database Kittes used. "See," Jack said. "Candy from a baby. This guy actually used his real name. We didn't even need to look for him." Jack shook his head. "I thought my last job would be a little tougher than this." He laughed and I smiled back, wondering where I was going to go after Jack was done as a Privateer.

Candy from a baby. Not really. Last job. Definitely.

Chapter 13

First to arrive at Norman Howard's hotel was Lata. She batted her eyes at Norman when he opened the hotel room door and he smiled at her. It seemed like a different smile than the one at the Black Rose. Like he might not be under her spell anymore? She shrugged it off. No time to worry about that. She leaned in close and kissed his cheek, making sure he could smell her perfume. He seemed to begin to melt towards her and she was satisfied he was still in her power.

"We have to hurry. I made the deal. I'm supposed to call and tell them where we will meet them for the exchange. I want to tell them the Black Rose so there are witnesses in case they try and pull something."

Norman looked nervous. "What do you mean, pull something?"

"Don't worry. They want what we have. They actually knew you had taken it. I told them 50 million. They didn't even flinch. I probably should have said 100." Lata laughed at the craziness of being so close to so much money.

"We need to get to the Black Rose. Then I will call them and tell them that's where we are meeting.

You and I stay apart so they won't know we are together. If they try any funny business, you use this." She reached into her bag and pulled out an electric blaster.

"Aren't these illegal for people to have?" Norman said, taking it from her.

"So is stealing secret inventions from Zoran." Lata said and Norman gave a little laugh as he hid the blaster. He handed the disk over to her. As she turned towards the door, she saw out of the corner of her eye, Norman slip something into his jacket pocket.

"What's that?" she asked.

Norman looked guilty. "Nothing much," he stammered. "Another invention of mine. It basically freezes everyone nearby for 15 minutes except for the person with the device and anyone you don't want frozen. See it works like this."

Norman took it from his pocket and showed her how it works. He was sweating and red in the face.

"Relax," Lata said. "If they try anything you can blast them. Let's leave that here. Just in case. Maybe they will want to buy that too."

Norman nodded and opened up the hotel wall safe and slipped it inside.

"Now, let's go." She took his arm and pulled him through the door.

At the street, they entered a jet-cab and told the driver to take them to the Black Rose. They didn't notice the car pulling just far enough behind them not to be seen following. That was me and Jack. He could barely control himself. I had never seen him this excited before. I have to admit. It was starting to make me a little nervous.

Jack and I were definitely off our game. He was excited. I was nervous. And neither of us noticed the jet-car that pulled out behind us. That's right. The one with Kittes, Vankenson and Blizzard in it. They followed us to the Black Rose. Talk about candy from a baby.

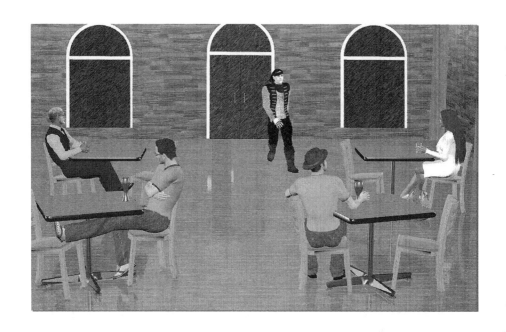

At the Black Rose, Lata sat down at a nice table (is there such a thing at the Black Rose?) facing the door so she could see everyone coming in. As they planned, Norman sat across the room at another table. Even excited as he was, Jack told me to go around and cover the back door.

That is when things started happening fast. Jack entered the Black Rose and saw first Lata, then Norman. He knew exactly what Norman looked like. First, the Volchinks had given us his picture. Second, he stuck out in the Black Rose since he was the only respectable looking customer in the place. Jack went right for Lata, keeping one eye on Norman.

"Hand over the disk," Jack told Lata.

"What are you talking about?" she said innocently.

"Don't cause a scene. No one needs to get hurt."

Lata looked over at Norman, begging him with her eyes to get out the blaster. Finally, he seemed to understand and started to fumble, taking out the gun. Jack turned in one swift movement and pointed one blaster at Norman and another at Lata. He was always fast on the draw, Jack was.

"Fork it over. Now. I won't ask again." Jack said.

Lata sighed and reached into her bag and removed the disk. "Thank-you," Jack smiled and started for the door. "And drop the blaster, please." He told Norman. Norman did so and came over to Lata as Jack headed for the back door where I was waiting outside.

Norman leaned over and whispered to Lata, "Don't worry. It's a fake. The real one is still at the hotel. I was worried something might go wrong."

Lata smiled. "Norman, you are a genius."

Just then, as if out of nowhere, Kittes, Vankenson and Blizzard appeared. "We'll take that," they told Jack just as he reached the door.

"No, you won't" Jack answered. He wasn't about to let anyone stop him from finishing this job. His dream job. His last job. I don't think he was thinking clearly. He reached for his laser blaster. But Blizzard was faster and he also carried a laser blaster. He blasted Jack, who fell to the floor in a clump. Just like that, the great Jack Lightsky was finished.

Kittes took the disk off of Jack's body. Vankenson grabbed Norman Howard by the collar like he was a stray dog. "You're coming with us." He said.

"Why," Norman stammered. "You have the disk."

"So you say," Kittes snarled. We'll check it out and see exactly what we have."

And off they went, disappearing as quickly as they had appeared. Lata was left at the table alone. Instead of her share of 50 million, she had Jack's lifeless body. But she knew what she had to do before Kittes and his friends discovered Norman's trick. She needed to get the real disk.

She got up and headed for the back door, stepping over Jack's body. That's when I came through the door. I had gotten worried that Jack's picking up the "candy" was taking a little too long. So I had come in to check on him.

I saw his body lying on the floor of the bar and I felt sick in the stomach. I remembered his words,

"last job" and I felt like I just wanted to lay down.
Jack was gone. It didn't even seem real. How
could that be? Some of the incredible spots -
hopeless spots - we had gotten out of flashed
through my mind. To be done in here - at the
Black Rose. It didn't seem possible.

Lata tried to push past me. I was blocking the
back door while I stared at Jack's body. "Excuse
me, please" she said. Something about how she
said it or how she looked made me think she had
something to do with what had happened here.

I grabbed her arm. "What's your hurry," I said. I
looked into her eyes and I felt a shock run through
me. She was incredibly beautiful. Completely out
of place at the Black Rose. I heard sirens in the
distance.

"How did this happen? Where's Norman Howard?"

"How do you know Norman Howard?" She turned those blue eyes on me and I was suddenly in her power. "Were you with him?" she nodded at Jack.

"Yes," I answered.

"Do you have a way to get off this planet?" Lata was nothing if not a quick thinker. She was well onto a new plan. And as usual, it included a guy totally bewildered by her looks. In this case, me.

"Yes, I think so" I said, thinking of Jack's ship. I guess it now belonged to me as much as anyone else.

"Then come with me. Quickly." The sirens were getting louder. She had my arm and guided me out the back door. I took one last look at Jack before the door closed behind me.

A five minute air cab ride later, we were at Norman's hotel. "We have to hurry" she told me as we entered his room. "We have to get out of here and to your ship before they figure out the disk they have is fake." Once they do, they will close air space and we'll never get off the planet."

"Can they do that?" I asked. "Close air space to an entire planet?"

Lata looked at me like I was the stupidest fool in the Known Universe. "They are Dr. Z and Dark Justice. They can do just about anything they want."

"Right" I said, feeling like the stupidest fool in the Known Universe.

"It must be in there." Lata pointed to the rooms' wall safe. "You can't get into that with an electric blaster."

"Not with an ordinary blaster. But you can with one of these." And I pulled out one of the totally illegal laser blasters given to Jack by Zoran.

"Where did you get that? Even most Volchinks don't have them." Lata looked at me and I felt her opinion of me start to change, at least a little. Maybe I wasn't the dumbest guy on the planet, after all.

"Stand back" I said as I blasted the safe wide open.

Sitting inside was a disk and what looked like a dial with a bunch of settings on it.

"What's that other thing?" I asked.

"I'll explain while we are on our way," she said, scooping both items up and into her handbag. "Let's get to your ship."

And so off we went to the Spaceport. I was dizzy the entire air-cab ride. I don't know if it was Lata's perfume, her eyes or her hair. Or the thought of Jack on the floor of the Black Rose. Or the thought of stealing from both Zoran and Dr. Z and Dark Justice at the same time. The whole thing seemed unreal. Like a crazy dream.

At the Spaceport we hurried aboard the ship and I

fired up the engines. I taxied out of the landing

dock. "Requesting clearance for take off," I

transmitted.

"Clearance denied," came back the control center

response. "Airspace is temporarily closed. Taxi

back to the dock and prepare for inspection."

"Got it. Will do." I answered.

"Will do?" Lata looked at me. "It's us they're looking for. We're too late. What will happen if we just ignore them?"

"They'll shoot us down before we even lift off. See those cannons?" I pointed to the huge lasers surrounding the spaceport, currently focused on us.

"Turn around immediately," came the control center command.

"Doing so" I responded and started turning the ship. As I turned, I was pressing some buttons on the control panel. And as we headed for the dock, we started picking up speed.

"What are you doing?" Lata said. "They'll shoot us."

I grabbed the lever and the ship lifted off, tilting at an angle. "They can't shoot what they can't see." I had cloaked our ship. We would be well clear of Vegastopia air space when the cloaking wore off.

In the control center, a nervous controller was on the transmitter with Kittes. "I don't know what happened sir. They disappeared. One minute they were there and the next there was just a black shadow."

"A black shadow!" Kittes slammed the receiver against the wall.

Dr. Z looked up from across the room. "What's the matter?" he asked.

"A black shadow has our disk," Kittes growled.

Chapter 14

And so two intergalactic space jumps later, we arrived on Prestis 3. How did we pick it? Just dumb luck I guess (get the sarcasm, right?). We were trying to get as far from Dr. Z and Dark Justice as possible and there was Prestis 3. It looked like a civilized place to get some food and figure out our next move. So we landed.

I was pretty much under Lata's spell. I know, I know. I had totally forgotten Jack's warning - advice. "Guys will do stupid things for a pretty girl. Guys will do very stupid things for very pretty girls."

One of the many stupid things I did was show Lata how to fly the ship while we were traveling. I was kind of showing off and I wasn't sure she was even listening. But she was.

Lata was busy coming up with a plan. She said we needed to find a way to get in touch with Kittes and Dr. Z and make a new deal. I thought about Jack's body on the floor of the Black Rose. For all his faults, Jack was the guy who had saved me and taught me the things I needed to get by in an unfriendly universe. They could have just taken the disk and let him live. Somehow, some way, I needed to make them pay for what they did. And not just with money.

"What about Norman Howard" I asked.

"What about him" Lata said. "There's nothing we can do for him. Maybe they will let him go if they get the disk."

"Trade the disk for him?" I asked. Lata looked at me like I had become the stupidest guy in the Universe again.

"No, but if we sell them the disk, they will probably let him go. What would they need him for then?"

What did they need to shoot Jack for, I thought. But I kept the thought to myself.

I realized we had one teensy- weensy problem when we pulled into the Prestis 3 Spaceport. I had no papers allowing me to travel within the Union. Jack had his Privateers pass and no one could bother us with that. But that was his, not mine and it was gone with him. Of course, Lata had a complete set of papers for herself. Maybe they were even authentic. I doubted it but they were better than what I had, which was nothing.

When I explained the problem to her, she came up with a plan right away. Looking back, it sort of seems like she had that plan in place all along.

She told me to take the disk and get a locker at the air train station and put it inside. Then come back to the Spaceport with the locker key. I know - can you believe it - she knew I would come back and not try to steal the disk.

She would deal with the authorities at the Spaceport as if this was her ship. I wouldn't need to show any papers and if they searched her or the ship, they wouldn't find the disk.

It seemed like as good a plan as any. She would have to pretend she had flown the ship but she figured she could do that now that I had shown her the basics. And I needed to get off the ship undetected. Spaceports are very busy places with lots of people about. So I figured I could handle that. Then all I needed to do was come back and meet her outside the Spaceport.

Well, I did my part. I hustled over to the air train station. I got a locker and put the disk inside. Then I hurried back to meet Lata at a cafe across from the Spaceport. She was sitting at an outside table, looking beautiful. She smiled and tossed her hair as I sat down.

"The key?" she whispered, putting her hand on top of mine. "Put it in my hand.'

I did as she asked. I wasn't sure why she was whispering until she withdrew her hand.

Two Prestis 3 officers stepped forward. One looked human. But one looked like a Rhino. "Your papers please sir," the human looking one of then said. The Rhino one clasped his hand on my shoulder and he was strong. I knew I wasn't going anywhere with that hand on me.

"I'm sorry" Lata mouthed the words silently as she got up and left the table.

The Rhino half lifted, half pushed me out of the cafe. All I could think of was Jack's advice and warning. And how I had forgotten it. You know it so I won't repeat it here. But then and there, I knew I had sure been as stupid as any guy ever.

* * * *

Enough of the past. To the present. The smelly, dark, dingy, depressing present of prison on Prestis 3. Rhino guards grunting as we shuffle by. Watery, tasteless (if we're lucky) gruel for meal after meal. And worst of all - three days until the transport to the prison planet. Three short days.

Every day that week, the oily little weasel of a

warden made a point of stopping by my cell.

"Smart-boy" he would call me. Or "Bright-boy."

Either way, the message was always the same:

"six days," then "five days," then "four," and today

it was three." He would smile that slimy insincere

smile. I would try and look as calm as possible.

Like I didn't have a care in the world. Who cares if

they are about to get shipped off to a prison planet

for a life sentence of back breaking labor with no chance to ever leave.

"How's the laundry business" I would smile. Or, "You have to get some new material."

Today, my flip response was "Pretty good at math, eh? Bet that helps with all the money you're stealing."

He tried to smile in response but I thought I saw I had hit a nerve. I saw him quickly glance at the Rhino guard before storming off. Was that a flicker of life in the Rhino's eyes?

It was a bright sunny day as we shuffled into the Yard. Tiny came over and mumbled "Three days. Only three days." He did not look calm at all.

I couldn't bring myself to fake it with Tiny. "I know Tine." I sighed.

And that's when it happened. The first thing we noticed was a strong wind suddenly blowing through the Yard. Then the sound of a ship engine way closer than it should be. Then a dark cloud as the ship descended. A voice came over the prison loudspeaker: "Everyone move to the rear of the Yard immediately."

I saw the Warden come out onto the balcony next to this office and look skyward. "What's the meaning of this?" he asked. "Is the Transport ship early?"

"My stomach sank as he said that. Tiny looked like he would cry. Our last precious three days, taken from us! But as the Rhino moved us out of

the way of the landing ship, the strangest thing

happened. Everyone in the Yard who I could see -

even the Warden on his balcony - froze. Except

me. I was so confused I thought I was dreaming.

As the ship landed, I recognized it. It couldn't be,

I thought. I felt a jolt of hope spread through me.

For the first time in a long time.

The hatch to the ship opened and the steps

unfolded. At the top, I saw a swirl of red.

The hatch opened and out stepped Lata. "Hurry up, she said, they won't stay frozen for much longer."

"Can you unfreeze him," I pointed to Tiny. "I can't leave without him."

"Terry, we don't have time. We'll try and come back for him." Even though she was saving me, I knew she was lying.

"I can't leave without him. Unfreeze him."

She shrugged and pointed the dial from Norman Howard's device at Tiny. He came to and looked around even more confused than I had been. While he was stammering, I saw a Rhino next to him had also been unfrozen. It just so happened it was our old friend with the red dot on his forehead.

The Rhino went for his weapon. I jumped forward to knock it from his hand just as he was about to shoot Tiny. That woke Tiny up. He reached over and swatted the Rhino with his fist, using all the power and anger he had stored up in the time he had been here. The red dot fell to the ground.

"Hurry," I said and we ran up the steps of the ship.

"What took you so long?" I said as we entered the ship and closed the door behind us. Lata just smiled. I sat at the controls and powered up, shifting into cloak mode.

"Bye-bye Prestis -3" I said. "It's been great. Let's do it again some time."

And off we went. As the ship soared into space, I thought to myself with a little smile: There are a lot of people who are going to be very sorry I got out of this prison.

THE END

(not really)

Made in the USA
Middletown, DE
21 November 2019